For Bria Lauren.—J.E.
To my dad, Koshiro, who had as many siblings as Toady.—K.Y.

STERLING CHILDREN'S BOOKS
New York

An Imprint of Sterling Publishing
1166 Avenue of the Americas
New York, NY 10036

ISBN 978-1-4549-1454-9

Distributed in Canada by Sterling Publishing
c/o Canadian Manda Group, 664 Annette Street
Toronto, Ontario, Canada M6S 2C8.
Distributed in the United Kingdom by GMC Distribution Services
Castle Place, 166 High Street, Lewes, East Sussex, England BN7 1XU
Distributed in Australia by Capricorn Link (Australia) Pty. Ltd.
P.O. Box 704, Windsor, NSW 2756, Australia

The art in this book was created digitally.
Design by Andrea Miller

For information about custom editions, special sales, and premium and corporate purchases,
please contact Sterling Special Sales at 800-805-5489 or specialsales@sterlingpublishing.com.

Manufactured in China
Lot #:
2 4 6 8 10 9 7 5 3 1
12/15

www.sterlingpublishing.com/kids

teeny tiny toady

BY Jill Esbaum

ILLUSTRATED BY Keika Yamaguchi

STERLING CHILDREN'S BOOKS

New York

Hopping faster than she ever
in her tiny life had hopped,
hurry-scurry, wild with worry,
Teeny flopped

and plopped

and slopped,

dodging spiderwebs and mushrooms,
leaping bugs and sluggy mothers,
till she skidded through the door—at last!—to gasp . . .

I need you, brothers!

"At the pond," she panted, frantic.
"There were people everywhere!
Mama's stuck inside a bucket!
Help me get her out of there!"

Brothers tumbled, bumble-jumble,
as they stumbled for the door.
"Don't you worry, kid. *We'll* save her!"
Off the seven toadies tore.

Teeny tried to keep from crying
as she scrabbled up the road,
wishing *she* could be a bigger, stronger,
hero kind of toad.

When she found her brothers
p-u-s-h-i-n-g
she rushed in to give a nudge.
Muscles popped and faces reddened. Still . . .
the bucket wouldn't budge.

Brothers put their heads together,
saying "Phooey" and "What now?"

From their ankles, Teeny wondered,
"Could we *lift* her out somehow?"

Someone bent way down . . . to listen?
No—to pat her on the head.
Then he swept her from the huddle,
"We can handle this," he said.

"Stand on shoulders!" someone shouted.
"Build a toady pyramid!"

It took lots of sweat (and twisting),
but eventually they did.

"Pleeeeease save her," Teeny pleaded.
Toadies s-t-r-e-t-c-h-e-d as best they could
till one wibbly-wobbly brother–oops!–
stretched farther than he should.

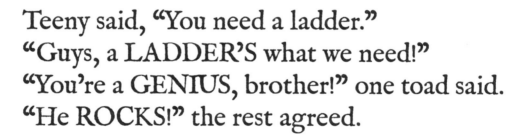

Teeny said, "You need a ladder."
"Guys, a LADDER'S what we need!"
"You're a GENIUS, brother!" one toad said.
"He ROCKS!" the rest agreed.

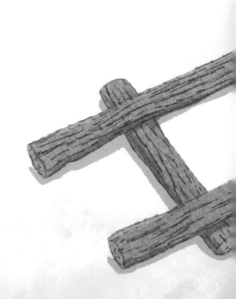

So they hurried to the pond
to gather reeds and bendy stuff.
Then they **looped**

and **lashed**

and **knotted**

till each rung felt strong enough.

As they climbed, their sister hollered,
"Won't you need some kind of rope?"
Did a single toady brother
pay attention to her?

Nope.

They just teetered on their tippytoes
around the bucket's top.
One said,
"Everybody *reach!*"

Uh-oh!

"What just happened?" Teeny stood there, blinking.
Rooted like a tree.
"*Now* who'll rescue everybody?
[Like she had a choice.] M-Me?"

"I'm too little," Teeny blubbered. "I can't do it! Not alone!"
But she had to, had to, *had* to.
Tiny Teeny,
on her own.

Teeny shivered as the wind picked up
and blew across the pond.
As she watched it flutter lily pads
and everything beyond,

an idea fluttered deep inside

her warty little head

till she chased it round

and pinned it down.

"I've got it!"

Teeny said.

So did Teeny's plan take muscles?

No, just brains and clever feet.

By the time the sun went down,

her rescue project was complete.

Up the ladder Teeny inched,
her bitsy heart a hopeful drum.
When she peered into the shadows,
Mama's voice:

"I knew you'd come!"

"Here's a kite I made," said Teeny. "Grab its tail and hang on tight." When it caught a gust, her family rose up into the light.

"I'm so proud," said Teeny's mama
with a big old smackeroo.
Seven brothers gathered round
to cheer and compliment her, too.

"Brilliant plan."
"We shoulda listened."
"You're a hero!"
"What a kid!"

"Wanna ride home on
my shoulders, Sis?"

She absolutely did!